W9-AWE-274

THE GREAT ESCAPE from CITY ZOO

TOHBY RIDDLE

Farrar, Straus and Giroux

New York

SOMERSET COUNTY LIBRARY
BRIDGEWATER, N. J. 08807

Particular thanks to Ian, Laura, Penny, Peter, and Sally

Copyright © 1997 by Tohby Riddle
All rights reserved
Distributed in Canada by Douglas & McIntyre Ltd.
First published in Australia by HarperCollins Publishers Ltd., 1997
Printed in Hong Kong
First American edition, 1999

Library of Congress Cataloging-in-Publication Data
Riddle, Tohby.
    The great escape from City Zoo / Tohby Riddle
        p.   cm.
    Summary: An anteater, an elephant, a turtle, and a flamingo break
out of City Zoo and, disguised as people, try to make a life for
themselves on the outside.
    ISBN 0-374-32776-9
    [1. Escapes—Fiction.   2. Zoos—Fiction.   3. Animals—Fiction.]
I. Title
PZ7.R4168Gr   1999
[E]—dc21   99-10645

There had been some strange goings-on at City Zoo for some time.
Something was brewing.

Then, under a full
moon, it happened.
An anteater, an elephant,
a turtle, and a flamingo
went over the wall.
They broke out of
City Zoo.

Their only contact on
the outside was a dog
down on the docks.
His name was McRover.
He took them in for
the night and gave them
hot soup.

At daybreak they moved on. Free as birds.

They wore disguises so
that no one would notice
them . . .

. . . so that they
could blend in.

Wherever they went.

But all the while, the Zookeepers were hot on their trail.

Back in City Zoo, stories of their escape were being celebrated in every cage. They had fast become heroes—the stuff of legends.

Though things were catching up with them—and they knew it.

They decided to jump
on a freight train heading
west, out of town.
All except the anteater,
who fancied his
chances in a big city.

He actually ended up living on the outside quite successfully—renting a tidy flat, and holding down a regular job . . .

. . . until the day he fainted outside a taxidermist's.
The incident came to the attention of the Zookeepers,
and within hours he was recaptured.

Meanwhile the elephant, the turtle, and the flamingo
were leaving the city farther and farther behind.

They took the train to the end of the line and picked up jobs out there, working on the railways.

Then people started asking questions and it was time to move on.

It was a similar story wherever they went.

So they took to the hills and built themselves a hideout,
making rare visits to the nearest town for provisions.

Things were finally working out . . .

But the elephant blew
it when he could no
longer resist the
fountain in town.

Sensing trouble, the turtle and the flamingo chose to evacuate.

Their best chance was to head for the border.

By whatever means.

Trouble eventually caught up with them
during a daring visit to a truck stop.
The turtle fell on his back and couldn't get up.

Like the others,
the recaptured turtle
returned to City Zoo
a hero.

And the flamingo?

Although there were
reports of unconfirmed
sightings,

no one knew if he was dead . . .

. . . or alive!

And so, to this day, the story of
the anteater, the elephant,
the turtle, and the flamingo is told,
passed down through generations
of animals, from cage to cage,
from zoo to zoo.

And though over time many versions
have arisen, some wildly exaggerated,
others plainly false, you will find
no truer account than this
of those extraordinary events
that surrounded
THE GREAT ESCAPE
FROM CITY ZOO.

THE END

3/00

Picture RIDDLE
Riddle, Tohby.
The great escape from City
 Zoo